High up on a cliff above the shimmering sea, there lived a family of swallows.

There were ten brothers and sisters:

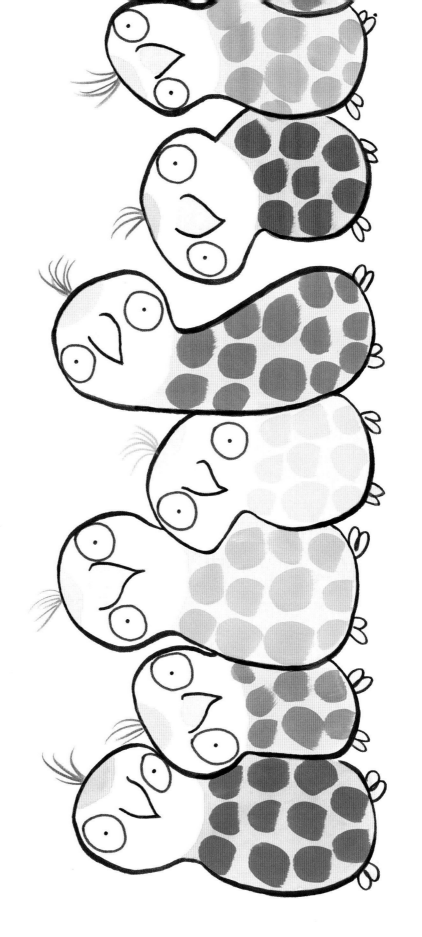

Edgar, Maude, Rupert, Helena, Winnie, Cecil Beatrix, Rosalie...

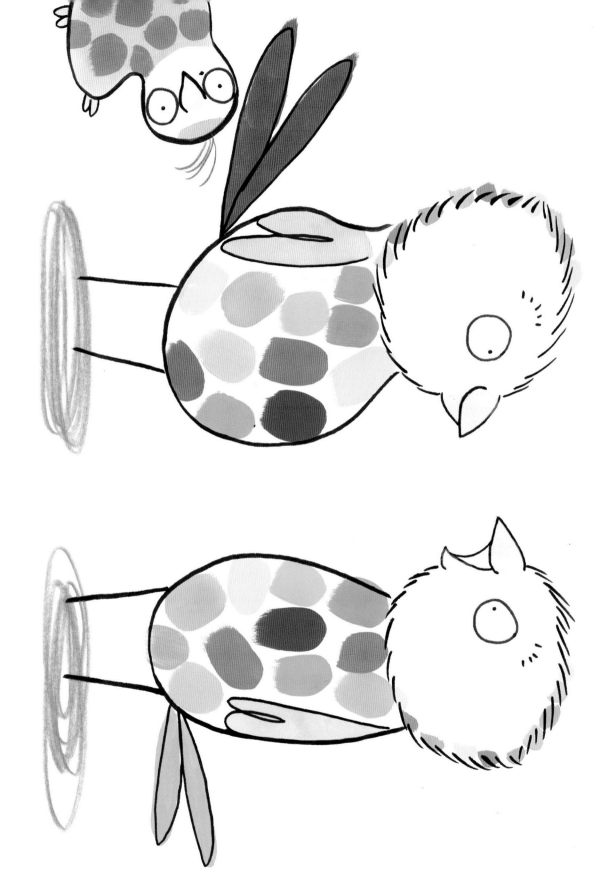

Pippi and Burt.

Each night,
big brother Burt
looked at the moon
while big sister
Pippi worried.

"This nest is
too SMALL!"
Pippi grumbled.

"A bigger nest would
have room for
Rupert's stinky feet...

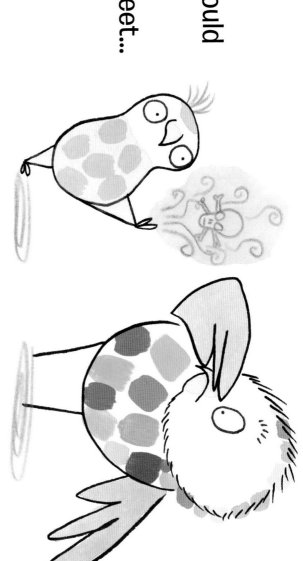

and Maude's judo...

and Cecil's band practice."

PHEEER ZWEE

"Well, the world is BIG and so are we," chirped Burt.

"Let's go and find somewhere BIG to live!"

So away they flew
into the night sky
to find a new place
to call home.

The next morning they found a spot that looked just right.

"This is PERFECT!" said Burt. "It's BIG and sturdy! I wonder if we could live here."

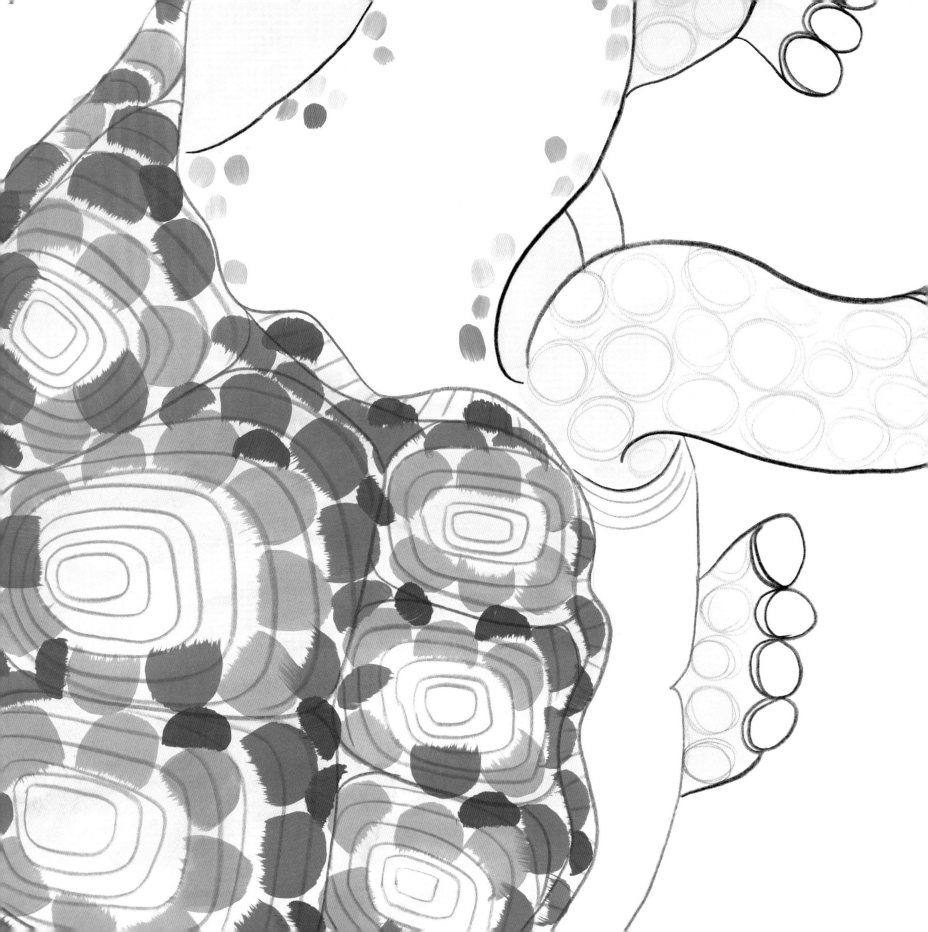

Suure yoouu caaan!

AAAAH!

"OH! That is VERY kind of you!" said Pippi.
"But I think perhaps we're looking for something a bit,
um, softer..."

The next time they were
more careful.

"This looks SO fluffy," sighed Pippi. "I wonder if we could live..."

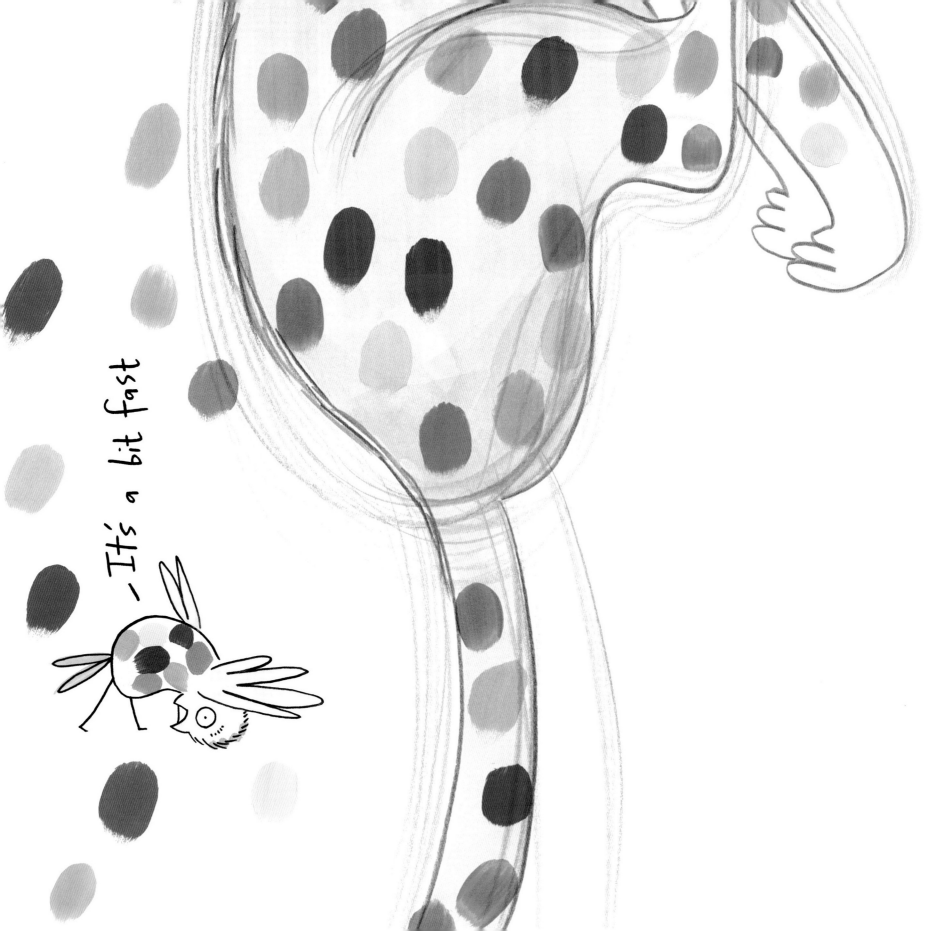

"Phew! That was close,"
squeaked Pippi.
"We were almost lunch."

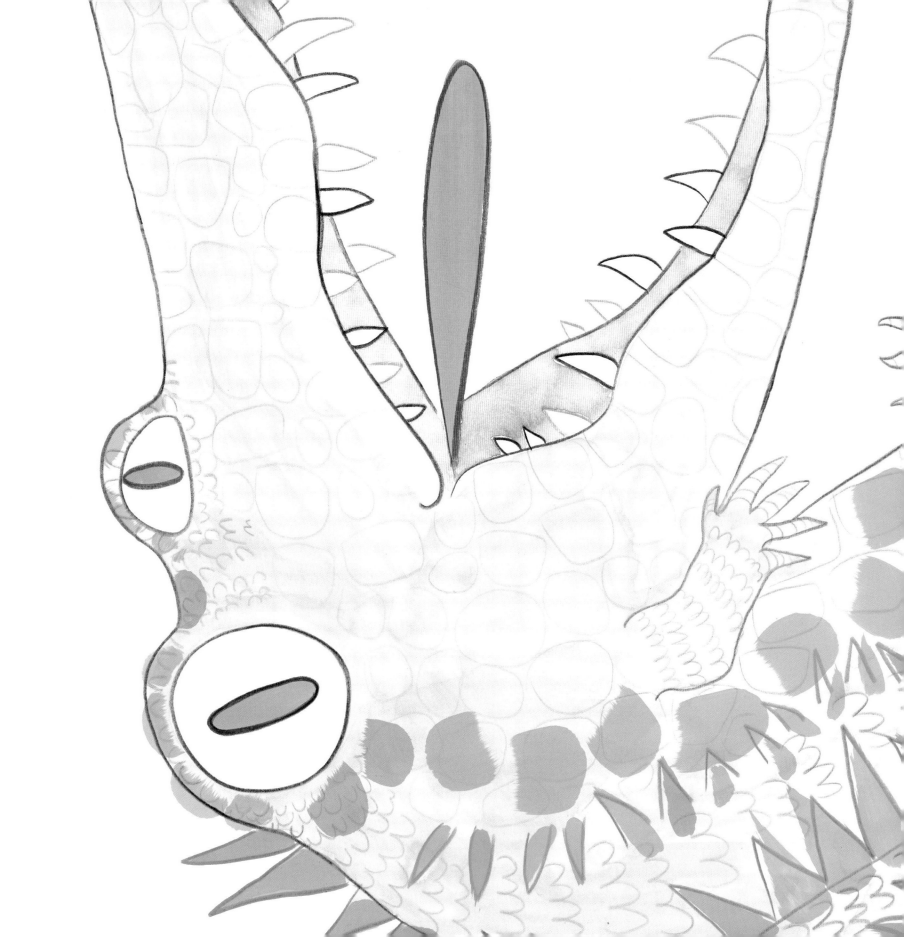

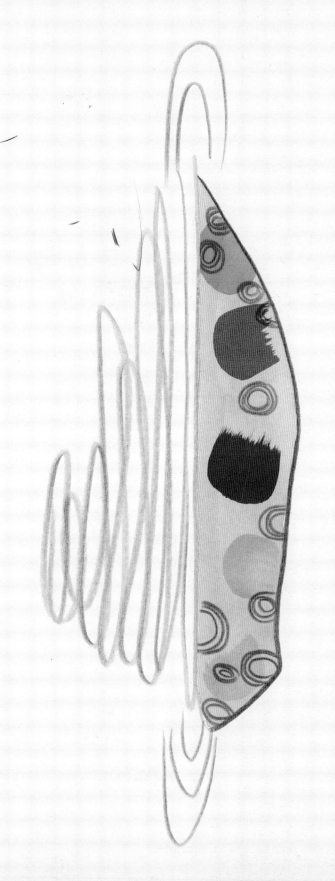

"Now, this looks PERFECT," chirped Burt.
"Not too hard, not too soft, and not too pointy."
"I've always wanted to live on an island!" said Pippi.

– How do you do?

"Can't we find somewhere that's not so big..."

"This isn't what I thought it would be," sighed Burt.

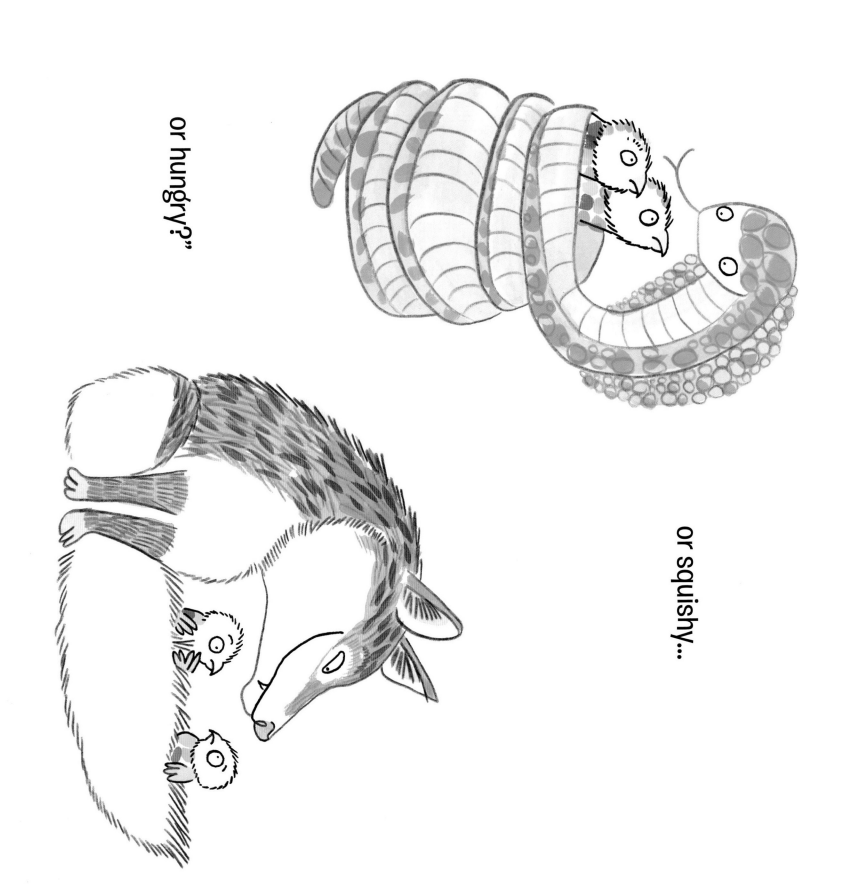

or hungry?"

or squishy...

"That's

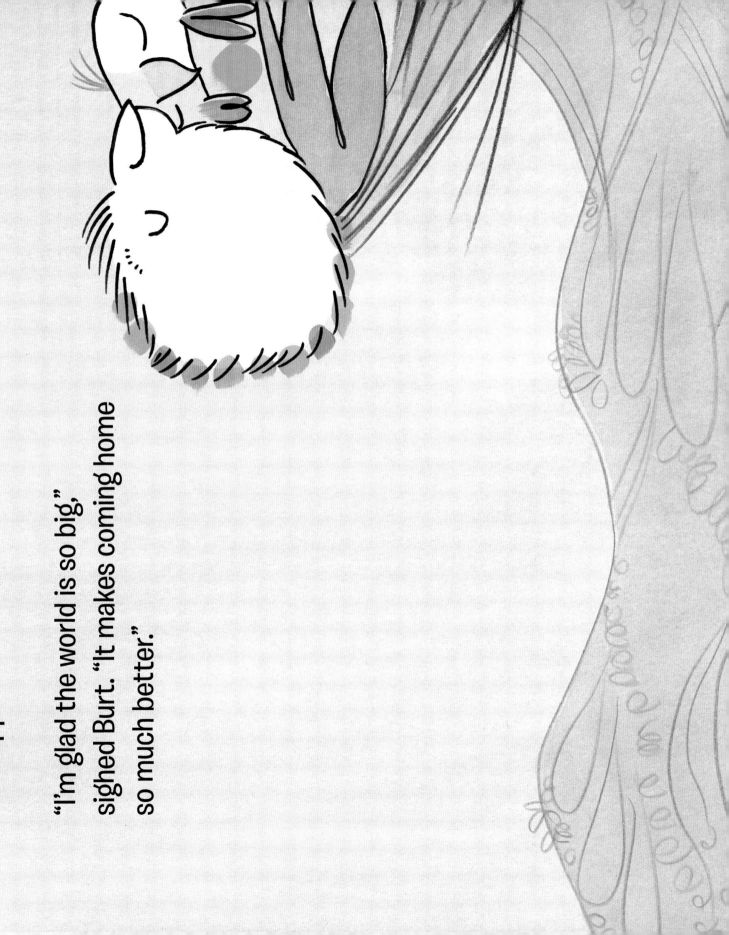

"Burt, you're a GENIUS!"
said Pippi.

"I'm glad the world is so big,"
sighed Burt. "It makes coming home
so much better."